Starring Katy

1st ed.

By Alyssa Satin Capucilli   Illustrated by Henry Cole

Ready-to-Read

SIMON SPOTLIGHT

New York   London   Toronto   Sydney

text of this work is revised from *Katy Duck, Center Stage*, and the art for this book is taken from *Katy Duck*, *Katy Duck Is a Caterpillar*, and *Katy Duck, Center Stage*.

For Peter, Laura, and Billy, my dancing stars!—A. S. C.

SIMON SPOTLIGHT
An imprint of Simon & Schuster Children's Publishing Division
1230 Avenue of the Americas, New York, New York 10020
Text copyright © 2011 by Alyssa Satin Capucilli
Illustrations copyright © 2007, 2008, 2009 by Henry Cole
The text of this work is revised from Katy Duck, Center Stage, and the art for this book is taken
from Katy Duck, Katy Duck Is a Caterpillar, and Katy Duck, Center Stage.
For information about special discounts for bulk purchases, please contact Simon & Schuster
Special Sales at 1-866-506-1949 or business@simonandschuster.com.
The Simon & Schuster Speakers Bureau can bring authors to your live event. For more
information or to book an event contact the Simon & Schuster Speakers Bureau at 1-866-248-3049
or visit our website at www.simonspeakers.com.
Manufactured in the United States of America 0214 LAK
10 9 8 7 6
Library of Congress Cataloging-in-Publication Data
Capucilli, Alyssa Satin, 1957-
Starring Katy Duck / by Alyssa Satin Capucilli ; illustrated by Henry Cole. — 1st Simon Spotlight
Ready-to-read ed.
p. cm. — (Ready-to-read)
Summary: Katy Duck is on stage and ready to perform at the dance show, but when the curtain
opens, she feels very shy.
ISBN 978-1-4424-1974-2 (pbk.)
ISBN 978-1-4424-1975-9 (hardcover)
[etc.]
[1. Dance—Fiction. 2. Ducks—Fiction. 3. Stage fright—Fiction.] I. Cole, Henry, 1955- ill. II. Title.
PZ7.C179St 2011
[E]—dc22
2011006190
ISBN 978-1-4424-3526-1 (eBook)

Katy Duck loves to dance. She loves to bend. She loves to twirl like a leaf. "Tra-la-la. Quack! Quack!"

Katy Duck loves to dance
in the morning.
She loves to dance in
the afternoon.

Most of all, Katy loves
to dance under a starry sky.
"Tra-la-la! Quack! Quack!"

Katy leaps and twirls.

Then Mrs. Duck says,

"Time for bed, Katy Duck."

Katy Duck dreams of
dancing on a great stage.
"Bravo!" cheers the crowd.
"Bravo, Katy Duck!"

The next day at dance class
Mr. Tutu says,
"I have a great surprise.
We are having a dance
show!"

Katy Duck is very excited.

She can hardly believe it.

What a dream come true!

"Tra-la-la! Quack! Quack!"

Each day, Katy and her class practice and practice.
They dance in the morning and in the afternoon.

Every night at home, Katy
dances under a starry sky.

At last it is time for
the big show!
There is a great stage.
There are pretty costumes.

"Places everyone!"

says Mr. Tutu.

"Take your places, please!

The show is about to begin."

The curtain opens.
There are bright lights.
There is an audience . . .
with lots of people.

Katy Duck feels shy.

Very shy.

"Tra-la-la! Gulp! Gulp!"

The music begins.

Katy Duck looks right.

The other dancers nod.

Katy Duck looks left.

Mr. Tutu smiles.

Then Katy Duck looks up.

The lights on the stage twinkle.

The lights look just like the starry sky!

Katy loves to dance under the starry sky.

Katy feels her arms
start to flutter.
Her feet begin to
pitter patter.

Katy Duck leaps and twirls!
She stretches and sways
to the music.

Dancing under the bright
lights is fun!

"Bravo!" cheers the crowd.

"Bravo, dancers!"

"Bravo, Katy Duck!"
says the crowd.
Dancing on the great stage
is just like Katy dreamed.

"Tra-la-la! Quack! Quack!
How I love to dance!"
says Katy Duck.